AF406168

GREEN STORIES FOR SUNDAY SCHOOL CHILDREN

GREEN STORIES FOR SUNDAY SCHOOL CHILDREN

Mathew Koshy Punnackad

Anne Susan Koshy

CHURCH OF SOUTH INDIA
2020

Green Stories for Sunday School Children - Jointly Published by the Rev. Dr. Ashish Amos of the Indian Society for Promoting Christian Knowledge (ISPCK), Post Box 1585, Kashmere Gate, Delhi-110006 and The Church of South India (CSI), Chennai.

© CSI, 2020

Email: csi.oikos@gmail.com

Mobile: 919847275754

All rights reserved. No part of this book may be reproduced or transmitted in any form or by any means, electronic, mechanical, photocopying, recording, or by any information storage and retrieval system, without the prior permission in writing from the publisher.

The views expressed in the book are those of the contributors and the publisher takes no responsibility for any of the statements.

Online Order: http://ispck.org.in/book.php

Also available on amazon.in

ISBN: 978-93-88945-55-4

Content Art Credit: Rashi Bhardwaj

Laser typeset by

ISPCK, Post Box 1585, 1654, Madarsa Road, Kashmere Gate, Delhi-110006 • *Tel:* 23866323

e-mail: ashish@ispck.org.in • ella@ispck.org.in
website: www.ispck.org.in

Contents

Acknowledgements

We are thankful to the Most Rev. Thomas K Oommen, Moderator of CSI, Rt. Rev. Vadappally Prasada Rao, Deputy Moderator, Rev. Dr. D. Rathnakara Sadananda, the General Secretary, Adv. Robert Bruce, the Treasurer and Rt. Rev. M. Joseph, Chairman of Synod Ecological Concerns Committee, for their steadfast support to the Department of Ecological Concerns. Also to all the Bishops of CSI for their moral support.

We have been enriched by the valuable suggestions of Rev. Dr. D. Rathanakara Sadananda, General Secretary of CSI Synod and also for writing an excellent preface.

We brought out Silent Rhythm, eco tales for Children in 2017. This book is out of stock now. This is our second book for Children. We would like to place on record our thanks to all the eco directors/conveners of the Dioceses and Synod ecological Committee, departmental staff Ms. Mary Stella and Mr. Noble Prince Sam. Thanks to ISPCK for the neat execution of the publication this book.

Prof. Dr. Mathew Koshy Punnackad
Prof. Dr. Anne Susan Koshy

Preface

With immense pleasure, I present the book 'Green Stories for Sunday School Children' written by Dr Mathew Koshy Punnackad and Dr Anne Susan Koshy. Sunday School is the best place to educate young Children about Christian values and inculcate in them an eco-spirituality for sustainable living from an eco-theological perspective.

The earth can be likened to a living organism. The different kinds of life forms, though different in their makeup, work together in a mutually beneficial way. The larger biosphere is made up of hundreds of unique ecosystems, which have different life forms that make communities specific to a particular region. Ecosystems vary in their size, complexity and their vulnerability to human intervention. Some ecosystems are very fragile like the great coral reefs, while others such as the hardwood forests of Appalachia are more resilient. All-natural ecosystems have four basic inherent principles:1. Diversity 2. Interconnectedness or Community 3. Regeneration 4. Interiority.

Diversity enhances the health and stability of ecosystems - "diversity is that dynamic within the evolutionary process that leads to an increasing complexity and variety of expressions." The sciences of biology, physics, and ecophysiology suggest that, greater the number of different life forms living in an ecosystem, healthier is that system. Diversity tends to make the ecosystem more adaptable, more resilient, and more stable. When diversity is eroded, the stability and sustainability of the eco-system declines dramatically.

All creatures in a given natural community are interconnected with one another and with the elements that sustain them. Creation functions as a living, maturing system. All that exists is interdependent and interrelated in an unbroken bond of communion. Virtually all living creatures interact with each other and the water, soil and air within the ecosystem. These interconnections comprise the central nervous system of the community, sending signals/messages, regulating interactions and maintaining the neighbourhood's overall health and adaptability.

Through the death and decay of plants and animals and the erosion of minerals, all material is recycled in the natural system, regenerating fertility and life. In a healthy ecosystem, none of this death is wasted, for it inevitability leads to new life or regeneration. In nature there is no trash or "waste." All dead tissue is composted into the soil and becomes the nutrients of new life. Along with the energy of the sun and the elements of the atmosphere, this regeneration process is what makes creation vibrant and sustainable.

All living creatures and natural elements have interiority, they are endowed by the Creator with both a sacredness and an integrity, a wisdom of their own. Interiority is that principle which recognizes that every being of the universe possesses a unique identity and integrity since everything is a revelation of the divine. Everything in nature is a face of God. Every being, from individual atoms to individual persons to individual solar systems to individual galaxies, has a non-material center, an inner intelligence.

Green Stories for Sunday School Children introduces these eco principles and the realities of the present world in story form to Children. It helps them to have a healthy, scientific outlook through observing nature by interrogation and reflection to understand the rhythm of creation. The authors introduce the vast world of environmental science from biblical and eco-spiritual perspectives. I am sure that the stories contained in this book will ignite the minds of children for a sustainable living. 'Green Stories for Sunday School Children' is a timely and commendable addition to the resource materials for Christian education.

Rev. Dr. D. Rathnakara Sadananda
General Secretary, CSI

PART - I

1

God saw that it was good

One evening Nisha was reading the Bible, "And God made the beast of the earth after his kind, and cattle after their kind, and everything that creepeth upon the earth after its kind, and God saw that it was good" (Gen 25). Angela commented "Aunty, I don't like these beasts and creeping things, they harm us. I don't know why God created such creatures". "That's not right, Angela, they don't harm us deliberately. It's only when we either frighten them or hurt them do they react in self-defence." "But honestly, I wish God hadn't created such creatures."

"Angela, these creations are also a part of the web of life. If any part of this web is broken, it will hurt nature and the natural rhythm will be disturbed."

"Aunty, what's this web of life?" "It is a natural chain, and one creature is dependent upon another for its existence. For instance, the frog eats the grasshopper, the snake eats the frogs, the eagles feed on snakes, the deer on green leaves, tiger feeds on deer, eagle on tiger, and when eagles die, they become food for beetles and worms".

"Now I've understood the web of life. But if one part disappears, what will be the adverse impact?"

"Yes, I'll tell you. I can illustrate it with several examples." Angela eagerly "Yes, please tell me, Aunty."

"This incident happened in Africa, where Hippopotamus existed in large numbers. A hippo on an average consumes fifty-two kilograms of grass, which meant that there was not enough grass for the cattle. So, people thought that if they get rid of all the hippos, the problem could be easily solved. So, they decided to kill all the hippos, and now the cattle had enough grass. But soon, another serious problem cropped up; the children in that area began to die because of protein deficiency. Immediately investigations were carried out and they got an interesting finding. The children regularly consumed 'thilopia' fish. But when the hippos were killed, 'thilopia' fish also disappeared, because the algae, on which the fish used to feed, began to decrease owing to lack of nourishment. The hippos used to rest in the water after feeding, so their dung became fertilizer for the algae. When the hippos were around, Africans got plenty of thilopia protein-rich fish. But when the hippos were killed the children also began to die because of protein deficiency."

"You said you have plenty of illustrations. Tell me some more."

"How many do you want to hear?"

"Two more."

"The next is an incident that occurred in Papua New Guinea island. To kill mosquitoes DDT was sprayed in the houses and the surrounding areas. Along with the mosquitoes, cats and lizards were also destroyed; consequently, the rats multiplied and destroyed the foodstuff. Eventually, they had to charter two aeroplanes of cats from Australia to solve the problem.

"It seems cats are VIPs."

"Not only cats but all creatures that help to maintain the ecological balance are VIPs."

"Aunty this is interesting. Tell me hear one more story".

'Let's take the next illustration from China. The Chinese used to see large flocks of sparrows visiting the wheat fields frequently. The farmers began to fear that this would affect their harvest, and so they killed all the sparrows. Now they felt that wheat production would increase. As expected, it increased the next year. But in the third year they found that the wheat plants were affected by pests. When the wheat plants sprouted the sparrows would catch the worms found on these plants. And when the plants' flowered it was the sparrows who protect them from worms, which would otherwise destroy the plants. The sparrows were doing a great job."

"Birds help us sustain life?"

"Yes, that's why after creating each creature, God found that it was good. In Acts 10:9-16 we find that in Peter's vision,

> *"About noon the following day as they were on their journey and approaching the city, Peter went up on the roof to pray. He became hungry and wanted something to eat, and while the meal was being prepared, he fell into a trance. He saw heaven opened and something like a large sheet being let down to earth by its four corners. It contained all kinds of four-footed animals, as well as reptiles and birds. Then a voice told him, "Get up, Peter. Kill and eat." "Surely not, Lord!" Peter replied. "I have never eaten anything impure or unclean." The voice spoke to him a second time, "Do not call anything impure that God has made clean." This happened three times, and immediately the sheet was taken back to heaven". "God did not create anything unclean. Every creature is a part of this web of life and it's our responsibility to take care of them".*

"Thank you, Aunty, I am enlightened."

2

Impact of Globalisation

Uncle Thomas of Dream Mount was popular with both the young and old alike. It was his art of narrating stories that endeared him to all; these stories were not just stories but dream stories. Maybe that's how the village earned the name Dream Mount. Uncle Thomas was not only well known in his community alone, but also popular in the nearby villages. People from the neighbourhood came to listen to his dreams and its interpretations.

The youngsters made fun of Uncle Thomas, "Dreams can never become realities". But he had an answer for that. In Genesis chapter 25, God gave his promises to Jacob through a dream. In Genesis Ch. 37, God gave his people clues regarding the future of Joseph in a dream. In Genesis Chapter 47, Pharaoh's dream was also a vision of the future. In the book of Daniel, Nebuchadnezzar's dream was also a prophecy of the future. The angel appeared to Joseph in a dream. Uncle Thomas firmly believed that if dreams are correctly interpreted, they will be the visions of the future. He felt that this was a divine gift as the interpretation of the dreams he had seen in the past was a revelation of God's will.

Way back in the nineties Uncle Thomas saw an unusual dream. As usual, he went to bed after reading the Bible. The Bible portion that he read that night was from Genesis the story of creation. Maybe because he had read and meditated on this portion, he dreamt something related to the creation story. He saw God coming down to the earth. There was a beautiful garden with different varieties of plants surrounded by other beautiful gardens separated by lakes and hills. God called Adam and Eve and told them, "This garden is very beautiful, and it has all that you need for food. You can work here and use everything in this garden. But don't desire other gardens.

Don't eat the red fruits that you see in the other gardens and don't plant those in excess in this garden." After God left, both Adam and Eve walked through their garden and found it was good. Then they looked around and saw that the other gardens were even more beautiful. They saw the red fruits and their mouths watered. As they stood there longing for the red fruit, a snake approached them and said, "if you eat that red fruit you will become like God, that is why God has forbidden you to eat that fruit." The snake tempted them with the red fruit and told them to destroy the barriers between the gardens and allow the seeds of the red fruit to grow in their garden as well.

At the moment, Uncle Thomas woke up, and he did not understand the meaning of his dream, moreover, it's not possible to interpret all dreams. King Nebuchnezer forgot his dream, and it was only through Daniel's vision that he was able to recall his dream.

Two years later, Uncle Thomas saw this same dream and the next part of the dream. The tree bearing the red fruit began to flourish and became a huge tree. But owing to its shade the growth of small plants was thwarted. Till then, different varieties of fruits and vegetables were available. But now only the red fruits were available in abundance.

God again appeared in the garden and called Adam and Eve, but this time they were afraid to come into his presence because they had disobeyed God. Eve told Adam to go into God's presence, and she would come later. Adam went into God's presence, but with an expression of guilt on his face. God disapproved of their actions and said, 'I gave you a garden with all that you required for a comfortable life, but in disobedience, you planted an exotic tree and destroyed everything." They remained silent. God accused them "You will not be able to enjoy the harvest of your agriculture or get a profit. You will be poverty-stricken.

Again Uncle Thomas woke up. But he could not recall the dream. Next year he still saw a similar dream.. Adam and Eve were in dire poverty, and they cried out to God. God heard their prayer, and he spoke to them, "I placed you in this garden to take care of it, and I also provided you with all that you required. But you broke my commandment and desired the other gardens. You planted the seeds of the red fruit (forbidden fruit) and destroyed your own garden." Eve attempted to justify their actions, "It was the snake that tempted us. The snake gave the fruits not only to us, but to the other gardens as well. Those red fruits can be seen in all the other gardens."

God then related an incident. "Once everyone joined together to build the tower of Babel. They wanted it to reach the sky and have authority over everything. This was against the will of God, and he destroyed it, and as a result, many languages, nations and cultures evolved. The attempt to propagate these red fruits in all the gardens is like the attempts made to build the tower of Babel. You suffered as a result of your disobedience to my commands. Now I have come to suggest alternatives in answer to your cry. You must boycott this tree, and if you abandon this inexpensive, tasty fruit for the more expensive and less tasty fruit, it will alleviate your sufferings to a certain extent."

At this point, Uncle Thomas woke up, but he could not understand the dream. But he felt that there was some meaning in the dream that he had seen then, so he began to pray to God to enable him to interpret the dream. Uncle Thomas began to read the newspapers and magazines in order to relate the dreams to the present-day context. He also shared this with his fellow human beings and social scientists. Finally, he had a revelation. He was able to interpret the dreams. He called together the learned people of the village and explained the dream to them.

This was Uncle Thomas's interpretations, "The gardens that I saw in my dreams are the different nations. Each nation has been provided with suitable food for its people according to its climatic conditions. India has been endowed with rich biodiversity. Adam and Eve represent the people, and the red fruit is the symbol of multinational companies. National companies cannot compete with multinational companies. The mass production by multinational companies will enable them to sell the products at a cheaper rate which will be a potential threat to the national companies. The snake that brought the red fruit represents the GATT treaty; because of this treaty agricultural products did not get profit. As the barrier between the nations was broken, it became easy to import and export commodities. The revelation is that poverty will increase."

Tiju, the Panchayat President, "we already know these things, there is no need for dreams to explain them." Uncle Thomas replied, "That's the last part of my dream. We must boycott all the commodities that have come into India because of the GATT treaty. Even if the products are more expensive and less attractive, we must decide to use only our products."

Kevin, an economics graduate caught the idea, "I will clarify that. Instead of drinking coco-cola, we must learn to drink tender coconut water or lemon juice. The companies that manufacture Coco-cola will lose its business. (Coco-cola has no nutritional value). The price of coconuts will go up, which will be beneficial to the local farmers. I will give you another example. We should manufacture and distribute bathing soap for our panchayat members. In this way, we can boycott the soap manufactured by multinational companies. The price of coconut oil will go up and through the local soap companies, many people will be employed, besides the multinational companies will not take away our profit. Moreover, we can use the profit for the development of our panchayat. There are many resources in our villages which we can tap."

Anjay, "What are the resources?"

Kevin, "India has the richest biodiversity in the world, which is our capital, that we have to protect and market. The Vicks formula was from the manuscript of Indian Rishis, but now the multinational companies are reaping the profit."

Tiju expressed his doubt, "All this is very costly, where can we find the funds for projects in this panchayat?"

Janakeeasuthram (People of the local body planning about the development projects) ought to fund such projects. "That's true we have enough funds, and it should be utilized fruitfully. If I had known this earlier, the funds allotted for

Janakyasuthranam would not have been wasted." Only if the villages are self – sufficient can we resist the adverse impacts of globalization and also all the villages must unite setting aside their political affiliations

> *"I have learnt this secret, so that anywhere, at any time, I am content, whether I am full or hungry, whether I have too much or too little". Philippians 4:12*

3

Use natural resources judiciously

Kurangumala is a small hill which was frequented by monkeys, and maybe that's how it got its name. Now no monkeys are to be seen, and it has become a small hill inhabited by people. Since most of the village inhabitants are foreign returned, it has an urban culture. Many wanted to buy houses and settle down in big cities, but they were compelled to live at Kurangumala as they did not wish to forsake the land of their forefathers. This thwarted desire was manifested in their modus operandi. They were highly disappointed that their dreams and expectations could not be realized in this rural set up. They wanted to change the name of their village to Monkey Mount City and transform the culture of the town into a western one.

Sunday is generally set apart as a day of worship for Christians. One Sunday during the church service Tiju happened to focus on floor of the church building. He felt that this was a shame as the present-day modern houses all have granite flooring. After the service Tiju shared this idea with his friend Mathew who also felt the same. So, they approached the Vicar.

Vicars are generally interested in church constructions and renovations and their primary concern when they take charge of a new parish is whether any new construction is possible, because only that will be remembered forever. In this parish, however, the new Vicar did not have to take any trouble to find out because the parishioners themselves came up with the demand of flooring renovation. Vicar said, "Tiju this seems to be God's will. Both of you must take the initiative for this. Next week, I will convene a general body meeting and entrust both of you with this work." Both were delighted that they were going to be popular in their church and village. They spread the news throughout the village and began building castles in the air.

But unfortunately, the church general body did not proceed smoothly as expected. The youth wing opposed the idea on three grounds and made their stand clear...1) There is nothing wrong with this flooring which is intact. Moreover, we use this church only for 2 – 3 hours a week.

2) Church renovation or building construction is not the primary mission of the church. Rs. One lakh set apart for this may be used profitably for social service, 3) Moreover, now sand mining has been prohibited, and it is not right for the church to use sand for renovation.

This was a great set back for Tiju and Mathew who had been dreaming of becoming stars with the proposed project. Anjay their rival, envious of their growing popularity wanted to oppose this, but having no points, he supported Kevin. Those who were reluctant to give donations now joined them, and this led to a great division in the church and the vicar was in a very delicate position.

Tiju whispered to Mathew "we can't go back on this controversial issue. This will affect us personally." He made certain strategic moves. He offered to donate 50% of the cost of removing the church flooring, and Mathew offered another 30%. The members soon began to shift loyalties. Some of them felt they did not have to contribute. They are going to beautify the church with someone's donations. So why should we worry." So, they supported the move. As most of the members were of the same opinion the Vicar decided to go ahead with the renovation.

The renovation began under the initiative of Tiju and Mathew and church politics also intensified. But the Vicar did not make any attempt for reconciliation now fully aware that for the smooth completion of the renovation there should be two groups with one group in full control. There was also no need for fund raising . Soon the renovation and polishing were over, and the dedication conducted with great pomp and show.

After the dedication, the Vicar announced that the members should not use footwear inside the church as the floor was newly polished. Kevin and his followers disobeyed this, whereas some remained neutral because they had arthritis and found it difficult to stand barefoot for two or three hours. Those who found it difficult to disobey began to bring newspapers. After the service, the sexton and the committee members had a tough time cleaning up. Meanwhile, another incident took place. One of the senior members slipped and fell while going for the communion. Kevin and his group took up this issue immediately and seized this opportunity to draft a petition to the Bishop pointing out that the corruption and demerits of the granite flooring.

Mathew suggested to carpet the church floor. But Thomas disapproved this pointing out that the granite flooring would not be seen if it is carpeted.

Meanwhile, church politics worsened, and the Bishop summoned the two groups to the his Office. Tiju's group highlighted all the good things that they had done for the parish. While Kevin's group accused them of corruption. The Bishop, after listening carefully to the two groups, remained silent for a while. Then pointing to his cassock, he asked them about the colour his cassock.

They responded immediately – "saffron."

"Who are the ones who generally use saffron robes?"

"Sanyasin's" was the response.

"Who are sanyasins?"

"Sanyasins are people who have renounced worldly life."

"Yes, the Bishop continued, "saffron cassock is a symbol which is symbolic of the activities and mission of the church and it is our task to fulfill it." The members began to feel that the Bishop was evading the issue. Tiju rather indignantly "Bishop, the issue is church construction and church politics and not the saffron robes of the bishop."

"Yes, that's exactly what I'm trying to say. We need a good building to pray and worship. There is nothing wrong in renovating the flooring of the church. But when we focus on that, we are likely to forget our real mission. Such matters are, in fact, a part of the consumeristic culture. We will not get real satisfaction if we focus on unnecessary extravagance. Real sacrifice is to say no to comforts even when we can afford it. That's what I expect my members to do. We must teach our members to use natural resources judiciously. Anjay was pleased "so Bishop our stand is right."

"I have not said that. If necessary, there is nothing wrong in renovating the floor. But that is not the primary mission of the church. Before renovating the floor, there are other areas that have to be renovated."

Tiju, "Which areas do you mean Thirumeni."

Thirumeni, "your hearts, if the hearts of both the groups were as clear as crystal, then there would not have been any church quarrels. You are a very hard-hearted people."

Both groups attempted to justify themselves. Anjay said, "Bishop their attempt to use the church to promote themselves was the cause of all the issues."

Tiju, "Their intention is basically to oppose all good things. They continued to accuse each other. Eventually, the Bishop opened the Bible and read out the portion about a prostitute being caught in the act and brought before Jesus by the Pharisees. According to the law, such a person should be stoned. Jesus quietly asked them, "what do you say?" Jesus quietly told them; the person who is not guilty of any sin should throw the first stone. One by one, all of them left. When the Bishop raised his head, the room was empty, except for the Vicar.

The Bishop told him; I'm not going to give any verdict on this issue. God will evaluate your ministry based on how you have been able to lead the people entrusted to you in the Christian way. Your mission is not to confine God in beautiful church buildings. The Bishop continued to read the Bible, and the Vicar too left quietly.

4

Do not pollute Rivers

Once on a visit to Japan, I had an opportunity to see the adverse impacts of water pollution on human lives caused by the dumping of pollutants into the ocean from the factory waste. This tragic incident that occurred at Minamata in Japan, not only adversely impacted aquatic life but also human beings. As this tragedy occurred in Minamata, this disease came to be known as Minamata disease.

One of the Minamata disease victims Hamamatho related his

sad story: "We are mostly fisherfolk, fishing and aquaculture being our main sources of livelihood. Initially, we did not pay heed to the grave changes in the sea – a great number of fishes began to die without any reason, and we didn't understand this tragic phenomenon. In 1955, when I was just nineteen, I experienced severe knee pain followed by numbness in my fingers and shivering, and on July 22, 1955, I consulted a doctor. As I complained of excessive fatigue, the doctor recommended rest and a good diet. According to the doctor's advice, I remained idle and ate raw fish from the sea, 'sanishi' our best food. But strangely the numbness and shivering only aggravated. I went for treatment to three different hospitals and finally ended up at Kumamoto University hospital.

Meanwhile, I had to give up fishing – my only source of livelihood. I joined Chiso factory on December 22nd, 1955, keeping my illness a secret. In the spring of 1956, this disease began to spread, and soon my relatives and neighbours also became victims. On May 1st, 1956, this disease caught the attention of the public, though the victims of this disease kept this a secret for fear of societal alienation. In August 1956, while serving in the factory, I was paralysed and admitted in Chiso hospital and later in Kumamoto University hospital. My father too became a victim of this disease, and I was upset. Soon my father died after acute suffering. From 1956 onwards, the victims and their families struggled with poverty and suffering and eventually succumbed to death. Many of the survivors who remained faced a bleak future."

Another lady shared her painful experience with me, "I am a fisherman's wife, living with my in-laws. My father-in-law became a victim of Minamata disease in 1957 and died in 1971, and my mother-in-law too became a victim and is undergoing treatment. I was born in 1929 and my husband in 1933. My husband too is a victim of Minamata disease. I had through him several pregnancies. My first child was born in 1948. She was a healthy child, but her child born in 1964 became a victim of this disease. My second child born in 1954 was a victim of this disease, and she died in 1956. The third time I delivered twins in 1956, one was stillborn, and the other died twelve days later. In 1957 I had a miscarriage, the next year I gave birth to my fifth child, who is alive, but mentally challenged. In 1960 I had yet another miscarriage. My sixth child was born in 1961 but died four days later. In 1962 I had another miscarriage. Though I'm not physically paralysed, I'm heartbroken and mentally shattered. I have no words to explain my deep sorrows and heartache. My experience is not an isolated one; it is but one among the many tragic experiences of several mothers and grandmother of my time. My only prayer is that you may not be affected by such tragic impacts of industrialization".

These tragic experiences shared by the two are only representative of a broader community who have been severely affected by the adverse impacts of water pollution and who have been denied a happy life and thus losing all hope for the future. This is the first incident in the world regarding water pollution.

All forms of pollution are wrong and sinful. The rivers, which are the sources of abundant life should never be polluted.

"And by the river upon the bank thereof, on this side and that side, shall grow all trees for meat, whose leaf shall not fade, neither shall the fruit there of be consumed; it shall bring forth new fruit according to his moths, because their waters they issued out of the sanctuary: and the fruit thereof shall be for meat and the leaf thereof for medicine".
Ezekiel 47:12

5

The Wise learn
from others' experiences

Anisa and Annette were good friends. Anisa built a new house with all the modern amenities and one day Annette decided to visit Anisa. Anisa was delighted by her friend's visit and proudly showed her around the house, Annette was much impressed by Anisa's modular kitchen. Anisa explained to Annette that she mostly used non-stick utensils (pans), as they were easy to clean and required very little oil for cooking, besides the food did not get burnt. 'Moreover' she added "nowadays everyone prefers to use non-stick pans."

Annette sadly, "My husband will not allow me to buy these pans. He claims that they are hazardous to health". But Anisa remonstrated, "Annette, we must deal with kitchen matters. You should not allow men to interfere in such matters." "Very true Anisa, but we have to acknowledge certain things and learn to distinguish between the good and the bad". Anisa disapprovingly, "Annette, I think I must speak to your husband. I think I will be able to convince him because I feel we must certainly utilize these modern amenities". Annette, "Anisa, you are most welcome". Annette's husband, Charles, was a renowned scientist. Annette was not sure that Anisa would be able to convince him. One day as promised, Anisa

reached Annette's house confident of imparting her progressive ideas to Charles. But Charles fully aware of the purpose of Anisa's visit calmly told her "All modern commodities have both merits and demerits. This applies to non-stick pans as well.".Anisa, "Sir, I have come to hear your arguments against the use of non-stick pans. I don't have anything personal against the use of these pans". "The controversy regarding the non-stick pans began with an article in a widely acclaimed science magazine Nature (19th June 2001). If you like, I will elaborate on that". "Yes, I would very much like to hear it."

"A polymer under the trade name 'Teflon' has been used in the making of non-stick pans. The name of the polymer is Poly Tetra Fluoro Ethylene (PTFE) a chemical. It is a type of plastic coating. This polymer is also used in electrical insulation tapes, motor vehicles engines, chemicals and frying pans. Homemakers prefer non-stick pans because food does not get burnt, easy cleaning and oil-free cooking are possible. Manufacturers have capitalized on this and are making a considerable profit. A great variety of non-stick pans are available in the market. But the real problem lies in the fact that the chemicals will enter the human food chain creating hormonal imbalance resulting in new diseases".

Anisa, "But why should they use such toxic materials to make these pans?" "I don't say it is toxic, but when heated it produces a poisonous chemical which is harmful to human health. It has been reported that birds die while breathing the gas produced during the heating of Teflon. Moreover, Teflon does not belong to a good family".

Anisa somewhat surprised, "Do chemicals also have families?" "Yes, like human beings, chemicals with similar properties are classified under one family or group. Pesticides like DDT, BHC, lindane etc. are classified as an organochlorine family. Chemicals belonging to Organo chlorine are like cousins". "Sir, it seems you are giving a lecture in chemistry. Can you tell me at least one demerit of this"?

"The chemicals belonging to the organochlorine family remain for years together. If this enters the human body, it will obstruct the functioning of the body and may even be transmitted to the next generation. Some may even obstruct the normal functioning of certain hormones resulting in certain fatal diseases".

Anisa sadly, "Sir, you mean to say that we must use traditional pots and pans. "What is good or bad is quite relative. These chemical relations differ from person to person; for some, it may be harmless for others it may lead to fatal diseases. It's better to maintain a traditional diet avoiding junk food. Anisa's dreams were shattered as she had to abandon her modern utensils. But in her shattered frame of mind, she seemed to hear a small inner voice "It's better to lead a healthy life rather than fall ill."Anisa felt that there was some truth in what Charles had said. This was a real set back for Anisa, who had dreamt of a modern home.As Anisa bid goodbye to Annette and Charles, these words came to her mind "The wise will learn from others' experiences, while fools will learn from their own experiences".

The wise inherit honour, but fools get only shame
Proverbs 3:35

6

Healthy Cooking

A group of students were listening to a talk on ecological issues delivered by an ecologist, Sunderlal. When the speech was over, Anjay got up and asked, "Sir, in your talk you said that aluminum is bad for health. Can you tell us more about that." "Yes, I'll explain. I said that using aluminum pots and pans for cooking is harmful to us. Being lightweight, attractive, available in all shapes and sizes, quick to heat and generally very convenient to handle, aluminum pots and pans are preferred by most women".

"If aluminum enters the human body in excess, initially it will result in memory loss, personality changes, loss of speech, sensation and lack of social interaction. As this illness advances, the affected person will not be able to recognize even family members. This illness is known as Alzheimer's. In 1907, a German neurologist Alois Alzheimer brought this disease to public attention, therefore this disease was named after him.

Alisa somewhat perplexed "Sir, how does aluminum enter the human body?" "Undoubtedly by using aluminum utensils for cooking." Alisa still perplexed, "How?" "I'll explain it with the help of a real example. In a childcare centre in England, all the children had constant diarrhea. The soup for the children was cooked in aluminum vessels. They changed the aluminum pan, and the problem was solved. When food is cooked in aluminum pans, a little aluminum mixes with the food and this enters the human body.

Now Anjay expressed a practical problem, "Sir, now aluminum utensils are widely used, and we cannot avoid them. Can you suggest an alternative"? "Yes, mud pots would be the best. Utensils made of pure iron, copper or alloy may also be used. Baby food should never be prepared in aluminum utensils. Similarly, acidic items like tamarind, tomato, vinegar, pickles, jams etc. should not be cooked or stored in aluminum pans, because chemical reactions will take place when acid mixes with aluminum'.

Alisa, "so if we don't make judicious use of aluminum utensils there is the danger of falling a victim to Alzheimer's Disease".

"She carefully watches everything in her household and suffers nothing from laziness. Her children rise up and call her blessed; her husband also, and he praises her." Proverbs 31:27-28

7

The Church's Response
to Terminator Seeds

The negative impacts of Terminator seeds were highlighted by a Filipino girl at an international conference where I was also a participant. "I belong to a particular Filipino community. We generally cultivated paddy using original paddy seeds kept for the purpose. As these seeds were edible quality seeds, we did not require pesticides or chemical fertilizers for cultivation. We produce enough paddy for food as well as seeds. A few years ago, an organization came to the Philippines. They claimed that they had high-quality seeds which would give an abundant harvest, but we were not ready to accept it. But they did not give up; they continued to tempt us by offering free seeds, pesticides and chemical fertilizers. A few of them yielded to their temptations and accepted their offer and began cultivation with the genetically modified seeds. Gradually the original sound quality seeds that required no pesticides and chemical fertilizers disappeared. When the organization realized this, they began to charge a nominal amount for the seeds, pesticides and chemical fertilizers on the pretext of the increasing demand from the farmers. There was no point in protesting, so they paid the nominal amount. The following year they began to extract the full amount. When we complained they came up with an alternative – they would

link them to the company from which they could avail loans that could be repaid at the time of harvest. As we were uneducated, we failed to see the underlying implications in their strategy. Year by year, the cost increased. In short, we soon became debtors, unable to repay the loans. Today, in our midst, there is no peace, only turmoil."

I did not then understand the full implication of this girl's story that I had heard years ago. It was only when I came to know about the terminator seed, that I realized its gravity. The farmer was losing his control over his seed, but the multinational companies were gaining the monopoly over it. In this technological era, most of the research in the agricultural sector is done under the cover of multinational companies, who only focus on profit. High-yielding seeds are produced through genetic engineering. If these seeds are readily available in the market, the companies will lose their monopoly over it. So, they decided to market only terminator seeds, which can be used only once, and the farmer will have to buy new seeds for each cultivation. Moreover, when terminator seeds are used in one region, there is the possibility that through cross-pollination the quality of the seeds of other plants will also be affected.

The popularizing of the terminator seeds throughout the world has become very easy as the export-import restriction have been lifted. Now in all types of cultivation, these terminator seeds have been introduced. In future, the fate of the farmer will be in the hands of multinational companies.

In this context, what should be the stand of the Christian churches on this vital issue? We can decide on whom we are going to support – the poverty-stricken farmer or the profit-making multinational companies. Many organizations are protesting against the introduction of terminator seeds in India. The stand that we take as a church will undoubtedly strengthen these protests.

> *And God said, "Behold, I have given you every plant yielding seed that is on the face of all the earth, and every tree with seed in its fruit. You shall have them for food. Genesis 1:29*

8

In Harmony with Nature

Most houses have beautiful gardens and roses are very common in these gardens. The roses in the garden invariably indicate the nature of the people dwelling there. If roses have big thorns, it suggests that the people living in the house adopt a hostile attitude to nature. We may wonder why rose plants are thorny. God made them thorny to protect the beautiful roses. Wild rose plants have bigger and sharper thorns. Whenever the rose plants are taken care of properly, it is very often noticed that the thorns will become smaller and softer.

As many will disagree with this observation, let me record specific experimental findings to prove this. In 1915 Sri. Manohar Barve visited Mandala where Lokmanya Tilak had been jailed for six years. The jail warden, a Muslim, told him, "Before Tilak's arrivals all the plants here were dry and unhealthy. But after his arrival, the plants became healthy and began to flower. But after he left the plants returned to their former state. Even though we watered and cared for the plants, there was no change". This clearly proves that plants can react to human emotions. Another story of an ayurvedic doctor who grew roses without thorns has also been recorded. Again, the story of Luther Barbanac, a botanist who grew cactus plants without thorns has been recorded. He claimed that he used to talk to his plants lovingly. 'You don't need to fear anyone, so why do you need thorns? I will take care of you." After a year the cactus shed its thorns. This means that if we talk to plants lovingly, though they may not understand our language they will feel our emotions.

Prof. T. N. Singh, who was a professor at Annamalai University, conducted several experiments which strengthen the above arguments. He wanted to find out the impact of music on plants. Every day he used to play the Violin for the plants. After a few weeks, the Balsam plants attained good growth and put on a lot of leaves. After conducting similar experiments on different kinds of plants, he concluded that harmonious sounds result in better growth, flowering and seed production. Prof. Singh further conducted identical experiments on paddy and found that music increased its yield. Music has influenced not only plants but also animals . There is a story of Ramana Maharshi in Tamilnadu, when he went walking his cattle and other pet animals accompanied him. When he reached the forest, the wild animals also joined him, and spent time together and later returned to their respective shelters. There is a mysterious power in the universe, which is beyond our five senses. According to the Christian church history, Francis of Assissi was a person who had this power. Animals were his friends, and he understood their languages.

The Bible calls for a harmonious co-existence with nature, which is only possible by a change in our attitude and lifestyle.

> *The wolf will live with the lamb, the leopard will lie down with the goat, the calf and the lion and the yearling[a] together; and a little child will lead them. The cow will feed with the bear, their young will lie down together, and the lion will eat straw like the ox. The infant will play near the cobra's den, and the young child will put its hand into the viper's nest. They will neither harm nor destroy on all my holy mountain, for the earth will be filled with the knowledge of the Lord as the waters cover the sea. Isaiah 11:6-9*

9

Groaning Creation

Anil Agarwal, an activist, who fought for a lifetime against ecological hazards eventually succumbed to death. At the age of 54, Agarwal died of cancer on January 2nd, 2002 reminding us that ecologically hostile and blind development of the present time will ultimately lead to death. The recent increase in the number of vehicles is the primary cause of atmospheric pollution, and it was Agarwal who predicted that in Delhi, where the pollution is highest, one out of seven persons would be a cancer patient.

Anil Agarwal a mechanical engineer started the NGO centre for science and environment and the fortnightly 'Down to Earth...' In 1986, the then Prime Minister Rajiv Gandhi, invited Agarwal to address the central ministers on Ecology and Development. Agarwal had the opportunity to address different committees of the Indian Parliament. The Indian Government honoured Agarwal with Padma Bhushan and Padmasrhee awards. It was through him and the organization that the concept of water harvesting to combat drought gained popularity. Moreover, it was Agarwal who inspired the Government to bring out CNG vehicles to reduce atmospheric pollution in Delhi.

Unfortunately, in 1994, Anil Agarwal fell a victim to cancer. In 1996 he published his story in Down to Earth. "I had never dreamt of writing any story as a victim of ecological

pollution. The term cancer is frightening, an incurable disease with a harrowing end. Even the poisonous treatment is a painful one. Just imagine your reaction if you are told that you are suffering from a rare type of cancer. In any case, that is just what happened. I was told that I had a tumour in my brain, which would gradually affect my eyesight, spinal cord leading to paralysis and eventually death. At that moment, I felt how merciful God is to those who die peacefully in their sleep.

I went to America for my treatment. They treated me with poisonous drugs to destroy the bad cells that affected my eyesight. Later they gave me an antidote for this poisonous drug. I thought I was completely cured, but in 1995 the cancer cells reappeared. The doctors suggested that I repeat the treatment, and I would get relief for perhaps another year. But I was unhappy and sought better treatment.

In modern science, the latest treatment was a bone marrow transplant. So, in 1996, I underwent a bone marrow transplant, and I temporarily felt that I had escaped from this fatal disease. However, let time decide. Meanwhile my only prayer was that some cure for cancer might be found.

You may doubt the relevance of a cancer patient's story in this context. But with my long experience as an ecological activist, I can say that my cancer is an impact of environmental pollution. I can evaluate things in this light of my articles, books and talks on ecological pollution.

We are generally under the impression that the adverse impacts of pollution will only affect the poor, while the rich will easily escape. But unfortunately, the learned souls of our country have forgotten a basic ecological fact – all the poisonous things that we discard will re-enter our body through air, water and food and soon we will become a victim of cancer.

"This is my story today, and perhaps it may be yours tomorrow." Five years after publishing this story, Agarwal lost hope and his struggles ended with his death.

The number of cancer patients is on the rise. To save ourselves from this dreadful disease, shouldn't we also join the struggle against this pollution. Let us pray for the liberation of our beautiful creation from the appalling impacts of atmospheric pollution.

> *For the creation waits with eager longing for the revealing of the sons of God. For the creation was subjected to futility, not willingly, but because of him who subjected it, in hope that the creation itself will be set free from its bondage to corruption and obtain the freedom of the glory of the children of God. For we know that the whole creation has been groaning together in the pains of childbirth until now. And not only the creation, but we ourselves, who have the first fruits of the Spirit, groan inwardly as we wait eagerly for adoption as sons, the redemption of our bodies. (Romans. 8:19-23).*

10

Contentment

"Owners' pride and neighbours' envy" is a television advertisement to exploit our emotions to market their goods. The company exploits our feelings to sell their goods. As an impact of globalization, companies are compelled to create an element of envy in the minds of people to market their luxury items. For marking gadget items like TV, Scooter, electronic gadgets, it has become imperative for companies to instill elements of envy in the minds of people which will compel them

to buy these items even at the cost of availing loans. If a man feels that he owns only second-grade gadgets, he will easily be envious of his neighbour who owns first-grade gadgets. This will compel him to get rid of his second-grade gadget and buy the first grade one. It becomes evident that the public is fooled easily because they forget the fact that first-grade items become second grade within six months and new models will appear in the market regularly. The company also ensures that the old model cannot be repaired, so the customer has no choice but to get rid of the old and buy a new model.

Envy leads to desire which in turn becomes greed, and one is compelled to avail loans to satisfy the greed. When a person sees better things, his greed naturally increases. Modern philosophy teaches people that one has to live in such a way that he will become his neighbour's envy. Such a lifestyle will undoubtedly lead to significant ecological problems. When consumerism increases naturally natural resources will be exploited and depleted, leading to environmental imbalance. Moreover, when the discarded second-grade products are destroyed, it will result in ecological pollution.

Plastic is another severe ecological issue that has resulted by the impact of Western throw away culture. These plastics which are discarded after single use cannot be burnt as they produce a carcinogenic substance called Dioxin, neither can it be buried in the soil as it is non-degradable nor thrown into the sea as it would harm aquatic life.

The love of money also creates ecological problems (Heb. 13:5). The apostle Paul advised the people of Corinth to learn the spirit of caring and loving rather than evoking envy in one's neighbours. (1 Cor 11:21).

Eastern philosophy advocates the sacrifice of all worldly comforts and saffron clothing becomes a symbol of this renunciation. A sanyasin who renounces the pleasures of this life and adopts saffron clothing is an example of this philosophic insight. Eastern church Bishops wear saffron cassocks with this perspective. In this philosophical perspective, this 'saffron thinking' does not evoke envy in one's neighbour. Ecology too favours such a lifestyle because it prevents the destruction of nature.

> *But godliness with contentment is great gain. For we brought nothing into the world, and we can take nothing out of it. But if we have food and clothing, we will be content with that. (1 Timothy 6:6-9)*

11

Anxiety for the morrow

God provided the Israelites with their day-to-day manna (food), and they were asked to take what was required for the day. Moses warned them not to preserve food for the next day. They disobeyed Moses and kept food for the next day, but that food went bad. They were anxious about the morrow, and it was this anxiety that caused their disobedience. Thus, saving for the morrow becomes an ecological issue. We have no right to exploit the natural resources on the pretext of preserving it for the future

generations. This sort of exploitation and accumulation reveals our lack of trust in God. The distribution of the water of river Kaveri will make this clear. The agricultural regions of Karnataka, Kerala and Tamil Nadu are nourished and replenished by the river Kaveri. The waters of this river are used for the 88 lakh hectares of agriculture of which fifty-six percent alone to Karnataka, forty to Tamil Nadu and three to Kerala. The river Kaveri is a 770 Km long river which has its source in the Western Ghats. The Kaveri flows through Karnataka to Tamil Nadu. Karnataka has checked the flow of the river with the dam. If it is opened Tamil Nadu will get enough water. When there is a decrease in rainfall, Karnataka is reluctant to give water to Tamil Nadu as they are afraid that their agriculture may be badly affected. Tamil Nadu too has a right to the Kaveri waters, but unfortunately, that is being exploited by Karnataka. Here also we see the same attitude of the Israelites. In this context, God's justice is beyond the vision of more for the more and less for the less becomes quite relevant. Water is for all, and it's nobody monopoly and all the regions through which it flows have the right to use it. So, to obstruct the free flow of the river is against the law of nature.

We see this same attitude (the logic of scarcity) in other areas too – the hoarding of food, looting of forest reserves, exploiting underground water, underground mining of natural resources in this basic philosophy that underlies all these anti-ecological activities.

In the case of nuclear weapons too, this holds true. It is this anxiety for the tomorrow that prompt most countries to accumulate modern weapons. Even if war does not break out, these nuclear projects in themselves will endanger life.

When we say the Lord's prayer "daily, we say give us this day over daily bread". But in reality we do not practice what we preach. Instead we assiduously gather tomorrow's food, today itself and create grave ecological problems.

> *And I brought you into a plentiful land to enjoy its fruits and its good things. But when you came in, you defiled my land and made my heritage an abomination. Jeremiah 2:7*

> *Is it not enough for you to feed on the good pasture, that you must tread down with your feet the rest of your pasture; and to drink of clear water, that you must muddy the rest of the water with your feet? Ezekiel 34:18*

> *But if anyone has the world's goods and sees his brother in need, yet closes his heart against him, how does God's love abide in him? Little children let us not love in word or talk but in deed and in truth. 1 John 3:17-18*

12

Francis of Assissi

Francis of Assissi looked upon all creatures as brothers and sisters. Once while Francis was going through a forest, he encountered a jackal, a ferocious animal. Francis tamed the jackal, preached the word of God and advised the jackal not to attack people. One day a fisherman presented Francis with a fresh fish (Karimeen), but Francis threw the fish back into the water. This fish in gratitude moved closer to Francis, and he preached the word of God to the fish.

On another occasion while Francis was delivering a sermon, due to the loud chirping of birds he was inaudible to his listeners. Francis ordered the birds to stop chirping and listen to his sermon. The birds obeyed and immediately fell silent. This Francis was none other than Francis of Assisi, the saint who is universally acknowledged as the patron saint of the poor as well as the mediator of ecologists. The creation was the medium through which Francis worshipped God. He firmly believed that when a person's heart is filled with God's love, his presence will bring peace to even wild animals.

Francis, through his saintly life, proved to the world that man is not the master of the whole creation. He revealed his humanity by addressing the other creatures as 'brothers' and 'sisters'. As he customarily said, "Brother sun gives us light, brother wind revives all the creatures with his strong wind, sister water is beneficial for us, brother fire brightens our nights (darkness)"

Francis offered a new dimension to the ecological perspective of the Bible. Francis' concept of universal Brotherhood was Christ-centred. Francis was able to see the divine in all creatures, which prompted him to consider all beings as his brother and sisters. When even trees had to be cut, he always advised them not to cut the tree completely, but leave the trunk so

that it may sprout again. From this, it becomes evident that animals' resort to attacking only when human beings attempt to have dominion over them. Similarly, when man ignores the silent rhythm of nature and abuses the soil, the earth will necessarily retaliate in the form of floods, earthquakes, landslides. If man illtreats animals, they too will be hostile to man.

The Bible gives us a vision of a golden age, where all the creatures of the world will live in harmony (Jeremiah). For the realization of this vision is required. A Christ-centred eco-version among Christians is the need of the hour, with a firm conviction that God has called us to be partners in this mission of bringing about this realization of a harmonious life 'when the lion and the lamb shall dwell together in harmony.

The wolf and the lamb will feed together, and the lion will eat straw like the ox, and dust will be the serpent's food. They will neither harm nor destroy on all my holy mountain," says LORD Isaiah 65:25

13

Do not Pollute the
Earth with detergents

Anju, "Anjana, do you know which is the best washing soap for washing clothes?"

Anjana, "Why". "We see several advertisements of many soaps and detergents in the newspaper, on TV and radio – detergents that claim ultra-whiteners, colour guard detergents and detergents that destroy bacteria. Is it true?"

"Anju if you want to find out why don't you ask the manufacturer."

"Anjana there's no use. As far as the manufacturers are concerned, they are only bothered about selling their products and making a big profit, that's their psychology."

Anju, "Then let's ask our science teacher."

"Okay, that would be the best." Both ran to their science teacher to clear their doubts," On seeing them, the science teacher asked, "Anju and Anjana why are you here?"

Anju, "Teacher, we have a doubt."

"Yes, come out with it."

"We want to hear about the soaps and detergents available in the market for washing clothes. There is a wide range of soaps and detergents. Which is the best?"

"Yes, it's good to be curious and express your doubts, boldly. In today's context to decide on what is good depends on evaluating how harmful it is to man and nature."

Anju, "Okay, we will put the question in another way. Are soaps and detergents harmful?"

"If you want to understand more about detergents you have to, first of all, understand the chemical reactions of both and how they work."

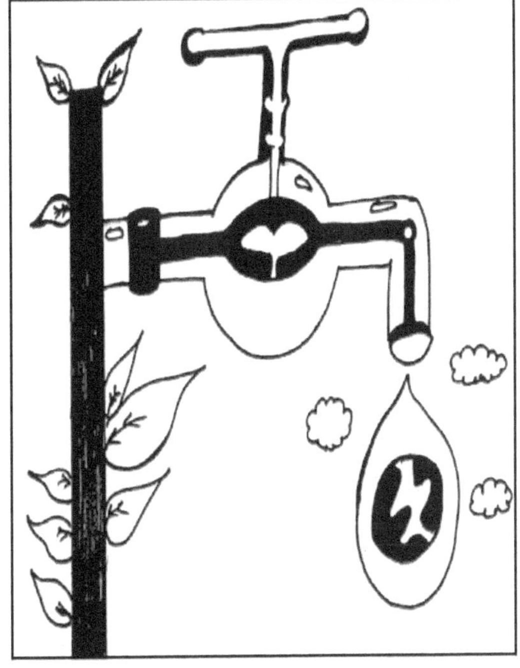

"That's precisely what we would like to know. Can you please enlighten us?"

"Yes, sure, I'll tell you. To make soap, we generally use coconut oil, sunflower oil, castor oil and other vegetable oils. Sometimes these oils are replaced by certain fatty substances. Soap in scientific terms is known as sodium salt of fatty acids. Soap manufacturers claim that the quality of the soap is determined by the colour and scent used."

Anjana wanted to know something else, "Sir, how do these soaps remove the dirt from the clothes?

Teacher, "I'll explain. Soaps generally have two components which help to remove both the dissolved and dissolvable dirt from the clothes. Both these components mix to form a thick mixture known as an emulsion. This becomes possible because the soap can decrease the surface tension of water."

"Sir, does the emulsion cause any ecological problems?"

"The elements from vegetable oil will destroy the microbes."

Anju, "Sir, what is the difference between soap and detergent."

"Both are similar in action, but soap is milder than detergent. During the first world war, there was an acute shortage of oils and fatty substances essential for making soap. An alternative had to be found and that led to the making of detergents. Surfactants are the chemicals that reduce the surface tension of water and remove the dirt from the clothes. This is a petroleum product. Linear Alkyl Benzene sulphonate was the surfactant that was commonly used. But today different types are used, and the companies claim that it is more powerful."

Anjana, "Sir, are there only surfactants in detergents?"

"Surfactants are the main components, but other similar chemicals may be added that may enhance the operating performance of the surfactants. Such chemicals are called additives."

Anju, "Sir, are these detergents hazardous?"

"Detergents are the best for cleaning clothes, but the residue that falls in the soil will remain for a long time and are non-biodegradable. Moreover, the phosphates that are present in the detergents are problematic."

"Sir, are these harmful phosphates used in soaps too?"

"No."Anjana, "Sir, can you explain how these phosphates create ecological problems."

"When phosphates enter the water bodies, it becomes fertilizers for the plants growing in water. When these plants grow it will take the oxygen from the water and owing to the lack of sufficient oxygen, the aquatic life will be destroyed."

"Sir, can't we make biodegradable detergents without using phosphates?"

"Experiments are being carried out, for that, until then I think it would be better to avoid detergents and use soaps instead of detergents to safeguard our health."

Both Anju and Anjana returned home happy that their doubts had been cleared and they had become enlightened.

PART - II

14

Marshes

I'm not beautiful, and I'm not interested in artificial beauty, but I'm contented with what I have. This may be precisely the reasons why people dislike me. Those who have a capitalistic outlook are trying to change me. I have not disclosed my name. I'm mostly land. I know that everyone views me with contempt, but that does not matter as it's due to prejudice. Waterlogged regions are known as marshes, and paddy fields are indeed marshes. Certain marshy areas are uncultivable, and some are waterlogged with dirty water filled with pests. That's the reasons why I'm not beautiful. It is, in fact, development that has made my position insecure. When paddy cultivation became unprofitable, paddy fields were levelled, and shopping complexes and flats built. If this sort of development continues, I doubt that I'll have any existence in future. But the truth is that I play a vital role for human existence. During the rainy season, I prevent the water from running off the land, and I filter the water and allow it to seep underground. During summer, when the water gets evaporated in some places, I still have water, and I supply water to the nearby wells and springs, thus preventing drinking water shortage. You will observe that where there are plenty of marshes, there will be no water shortage.

Different varieties of chemicals are used on the land, and some are very toxic. When it rains all this flows into the marshy areas, otherwise, if the poisonous chemicals reach the water bodies directly, it will affect the water creatures, and through the fish, it will enter the human beings. It is here that I

become significant I act as a filter, filtering the metal and chemicals from the flowing water. The flowing water reaches the sea only through the marshes. That's why scientists call us nature's kidneys.

Efforts are being made globally to protect biodiversity. There are unique microbes and plants in marshy areas, so we are known as the storehouses of biodiversity, so when scientists who research on biodiversity come to us, we are delighted.

We have an international organization to protect us known as Ramsar convention. Marshes got attention at that international conference held at Ramsar in India in 1971. The conference declared that wetlands have a vital role to play in maintaining the eco-balance. It is man's indifference and contempt of marshes that provoked me to say all this, don't be prejudiced. Each object in nature has a part to play in sustaining this eco-balance and protecting nature. It is this contribution of the great and the small that makes our life possible. Therefore, don't condemn us.

15

Neither Friend nor Enemy

I have more enemies than friends because I know for certain that the number of enemies is increasing. You may say that it is because of my actions, but that's not right. If you had understood me correctly, you will not accuse me. Let me explain about myself and my unique experiences.

I was born in 1873, but I became popular only in 1939. It was in 1948 that the Nobel Laureate Paul Mueller, a scientist who explained to the world about my role, increased my reputation. I was welcomed all over the world, and I was really awed by the reception that all the governments of the world extended to me. I became very proud and reveled in my glory for several years. The proverb, 'pride goes before a fall" was proved true in my case. Soon the number of my enemies began increasing. But, you are responsible. At a point of time you made me famous but today you are trying to suppress me. Had you understood the dangers involved right from the beginning, this would not have happened. I'm sure you are curious to know who I am. I am called DDT (pesticide). After the second world war, I was known as the farmer's friend because I appeared at a time when the farmers were in trouble with the pests, and I saved them by fighting against these pests. Moreover, scientists discovered that I was good at fighting against Malaria and therefore, more and more countries began to make use of me. I was not only the farmers' friend, but also became the saviour of humanity.

My misfortunes started with the publication of Rachel Carson's masterpiece

'Silent Spring' in 1962. Rachel Carson, who died in 1964 at the age of fifty-six of breast cancer, became the founder of the ecological movements. I am the main character in the book 'Silent Spring'. She explained how my family members and I are a threat to the environmental balance. Once the book gained popularity, I became an enemy of all the ecological activists. Though, I had been acclaimed as their saviour, now I have become their destroyer. I have also been banned in some countries because the environmental activists claimed that nature can be protected only if my family members and I are annihilated.

I will explain the arguments raised against me and my family. Although there are different types of pesticides, I would prefer to call my family organo chorine pesticides. My family members are called by different names – Aldrin, BHC, Chlordane, Dictol Dictdrin, Endosulfan, Endrin, Heptachlor, Lindane etc. Sometimes they are known by other names given by the pharmaceutical companies. Our sole task is to destroy pests, but we will continue to remain for years. Rain and wind will keep on transferring us from place to place. During monsoons, I will reach the lakes, rivers and seas, sometimes I will enter the human food chain through the fishes. Small amounts of DDT will not be harmful to human beings. When I enter the human body, I will deposit myself in the fatty areas, when this deposit reaches a level, the body cells will begin to increase to resist my infection. These increased body cells form a tumour which if not removed at the right time, will lead to cancer.

The greatest number of breast cancer cases is reported in Lancashire in England. In the agricultural sector of Lancashire, Lindane, one of my variants had been widely used, so then Lindane was the culprit. When Lindane was banned, I was taken up. If my character is known correctly, people will use me judiciously. Because I remain for years, I am a potential threat to all living creatures and humanity. If I'm not used cautiously, I will become a destroyer.

Recently a woman took me home to get rid of ants. She sprinkled me in the kitchen, and as desired, I destroyed all the ants. In the past, I was so powerful that I killed all the pests, but twenty or thirty years later, I could not destroy all the pests. By 1984 according to scientists the number of pests that could not be killed increased to 477, which meant that pests were getting immune to pesticides. Today DDT will not get rid of pests completely. The ants that survive had traces of DDT on them. They transfer it to the sugar which entered the human body through the tea, coffee etc. This old lady was quite unaware of the dangerous implications of DDT; she brought me home to kill her ants, but I made her a cancer patient.

This story is about how I who began as a saviour of human beings became their destroyer. I'm neither a saviour nor an assassin. It is humans who are responsible for all this, and even my friends have become my enemies. Therefore, my humble request is that you should call me only if it's necessary and that too only after you have understood the dangerous implications of using me. As far as possible it's best to avoid me because I don't want to make you cancer patients or destroy nature, I'm neither your friend nor enemy. All my variants are equally harmful, so banning me alone will not solve the problem.

16

Harmless - if in the right place

The truth is that you cannot live without me, because I'm everywhere. Even when you look at me with much contempt rout, I'm there too. I am both good and bad. I'm widely used in modern science and technology. Those who have me in excess become terminally ill and succumb to death.

I am silica and am present in mud and rock. I am second in importance in this world after oxygen. I have both silicon and oxygen in me. In 1984, a scientist separated this silicon, and with this, I gained dignity because, for centuries, I have been looked down upon. But now I'm proud because silicon plays a vital role in electronics. Some consider me a little mud, but others value me as a treasure. Everything depends on the way you look at me. Not only in the field of electrons but in other areas too, I have become an integral part. Without mud and stone, nothing can be done. In urbanization I have a pivotal role to play.

Labourers are in close contact with me, especially those who earn their livelihood by using me. I become harmful to those who work with sand, wells, sandpaper etc. In the course of their work, small particles of silica enter the lungs and block the air passage. After several months this will lead to fibrosis and eventually result in silicosis, which is a fatal disease. In this state, there is a risk of severe ailments like lung disorder, heart attack or cancer. Particularly labourers who work in the soil or stone quarries for more than three years continuously are prone to silicosis. Symptoms of this

disease will appear only after ten or fifteen years. In America every year, almost 250 people die of silicosis. Although it's not possible to abandon these jobs because of the fear of silicosis, certain precautions can be taken to reduce the risk of contracting this disease. Sprinkling water, so that dust particles do not rise, wearing suitable clothes, masks and going for regular health checkups are some of the solutions.

The truth is that I have no intention to make you sick. If you become careless in controlling pollution, that's when

I become problematic. I mix with the dust that enters the atmosphere, and you breathe it in, and this enters your lungs and creates problems. So, who is the real culprit? If you are careful, you need not regret. If I'm allowed to remain where I should, I will not cause any problem. Everything in nature has a place, if that is upset, then nature will react.

17

Biodiversity

The new generation may not be familiar with me. I belong to a category that is fast disappearing. Some people are suspicious of me, so it's better that I introduce myself to avoid further misunderstanding. I am a sacred groove, (Kavu) maybe it's because I'm a part of Hindu culture that people generally view me with suspicion. No one attempts to see the good in me, and they fail to see the truth because they are prejudiced.

I perform a very significant task as I am the lungs of the village purifying and

improving the quality of air. The excess carbon dioxide is used by plants for the preparation of food while the remaining oxygen is released into the atmosphere. An attempt on the global level is being made to protect biodiversity, as all living creatures in this world have a vital role to play in maintaining the ecological balance. Therefore, we should protect them from becoming extinct. Rare and valuable plants and animals have become extinct. It is this insight that all these animal and plants should not become extinct that underlies the protection of biodiversity. Noah in the Bible is the first ecologist to introduce this idea of the protection of biodiversity. Before the flood that came to destroy the world, Noah built an ark and took in all the species, both male and female. In this way of life, all the species were preserved.

Today, I'm known as the protector of biodiversity. Each saved groove is a rich heritage of biodiversity. Some sacred grooves are known as sacred snake grooves, which are virgin lands untouched by human beings. The wells and pools near these grooves which never dry up even in summer are nature's gift. The big trees and plants in the grooves increase the water absorption of the soil in this area, moreover, the dense growth of plants and shrubs act as an umbrella protecting the groove from evaporation due to sunlight. So even during the severe drought, there is enough water in the nearby pools and wells.

Today forests are valued only from a commercial perspective. When large scale felling of trees began, grooves and birds disappeared, and the natural control of pests was disrupted and mosquitoes, beetles etc. began to infest agricultural lands. To get rid of pests farmers were compelled to use pesticides on a large scale. But unfortunately, the pests started to outlive these pesticides and eventually enter the food chain resulting in fatal diseases and water sources began to dry up, resulting in acute water scarcity.

Why did all this happen? Only because humans failed to understand the ecological balance. My friends open your eyes and view things without bias, and you will reap the benefits. I'm your friend, and you must protect me.

18

I am harmless

Most people disapprove of me, mainly because I have been featured as a very harmful person by the media. To speak the truth, I am not as dangerous as they claim, for its human nature not to highlight the positive aspects. This is true in my case too. Please listen to my story without any prejudice and then decide for yourself.

I am generally known as Coliform bacteria. You may not know the others who belong to my family. But you must have read about me in the newspapers, especially in association with water. According to science, if I'm present in water, then it is unsuitable for drinking. There is a general misconception that bacteria are harmful and disease-causing. But that is not true, because there are both harmful as well as harmless bacteria. The harmless bacteria are actually essential for us. Don't be surprised when I say that I belong to this category. I am present in the stomach of all living creatures, and my presence is essential for digestion. Now you can decide whether I'm your friend or enemy. The controversies raging about me are due to lack of proper understanding.

Recently, I have gained popularity regarding the pollution of the River Pamba. As the Sabarimala pilgrims use the riverbanks as toilets, the rate of coliform bacteria seems to be increasing. I help in digestion, and I come out through the human faeces, which mixes with the water. When the level of Coliform bacteria increases, the media will immediately report that river Pampa is contaminated, because reporters are always in search of sensational news. Do you think the mob will keep quiet if the river water used for drinking and agriculture is polluted? The fact is that the media has not understood me correctly.

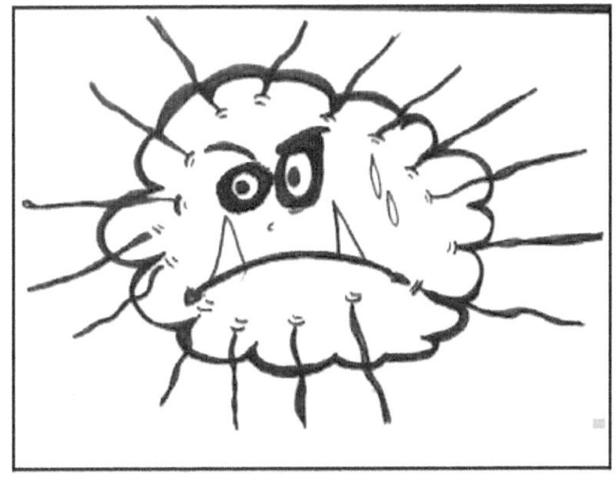

I am innocent and harmless, and I know it's difficult for you to believe this. I would like to explain how I became a culprit. I'm not the real culprit, but in reality, my friends for who's sake I'm blamed. A few of my friends are problematic. They are disease-causing bacteria, even scientists are afraid to examine them. The scientists discovered a means to deal with them. These dangerous microbes live under my shelter, when my number increases, they multiply, when I decrease, they too will decrease. As it's difficult for them to determine the exact number of those microbes, they present me as the yardstick of water pollution.

Now, I hope now you have understood how harmless I am. I will introduce you to some of my problematic friends – giardia and cryptosporidium. Giardia microbes cause stomach ailments called **giardiasis** – diarrhea, stomachache, and gas trouble are symptoms of this. Cryptosporidiosis in the disease caused by cryptosporidium microbes, Diarrhea, weight loss, stomachache are the usual symptoms which will continue for a long time and they become fatal. Research studies reveal that no suitable medicine has been found so far.

My friends are dangerous. It's is not possible to determine their number. Hence, when my numbers increase, automatically my friend's numbers will also increase. For safer reasons, the purity of water is measured in terms of my number. When my level increases, chlorine gas or bleaching powder is used. My story will end if chlorine gas is passed through the water for a long time, but my friends cannot be destroyed, they will somehow enter the human body. Though it's not right to deceive my friend I will tell you a secret to get rid of them. It's an ancient method – to drink only boiled water; when water boils, my friends and I will be destroyed. But when water boils, it will lose its taste. If taste matters, then my friends will be frequent visitors to your stomach and create problems.

19

Silent Killer

I don't hate anyone, and therefore I have no enemies. I firmly attach myself to some people, but unfortunately this intimacy puts their life in danger. That may be the reason why I am called a silent killer

You may wonder who I am. I am smoke – the silent killer. Yes, I am the thick dark smoke that is emitted from chimneys and pipes and spreads through the atmosphere. The smoke will become thicker when there is less oxygen, and things don't burn completely. Usually, I'm seen from the chimney of houses, exhaust of motor vehicles and chimney pipes of factories. The reason why the factories have very tall chimney pipes is that smoke causes great harm to human health.

The idea that smoke is harmless is a misconception because there are many harmful chemicals in me. Whenever anything burns, carbon monoxide, which is toxic is produced. Motor vehicles emit chemicals like hydrocarbons, nitrogen oxides, sulphur dioxide, lead benzopyrene, when this meets sunlight, many other dangerous chemicals are produced. When I go out through the incinerator in the hospitals, I come out with a very harmful chemical known as dioxin. The chemicals will change according to the place I come from. Global warming, which is a very serious ecological issue, is caused by the increase in carbon dioxide.

I'll explain how these different chemicals will harm you. Hemoglobin prefers carbon monoxide to oxygen,

and a chemical carboxyhemoglobin is produced. Once this happens, it cannot take in oxygen and the symptoms like headache, breathing difficulty, vomiting, weakening of muscles, dizziness, fatigue etc. appear. When the amount of carboxyhemoglobin exceeds fifty percent, it will become fatal. Lead that is emitted from petrol will damage the nervous system.

According to reporters, people who live at junctions face a lot of health hazards. It's mainly at these junctions that vehicles lower their speed and wait for traffic signals and it is during this time that I enter these houses unbidden. Because of this kind of air pollution people in international cities like Bangkok wear oxygen masks. Earlier people did not take much note of me, but I'm waiting for the time when they'll be afraid of me. There is no doubt that the supreme court has understood my threat and issued many orders against smoke air pollutions. The court has ordered that in Delhi vehicles should run on CNG to reduce air pollution. The motor vehicle department has initiated steps to eliminate me, so my expectation is on those who break the rules fully aware that I am a silent killer; they are not afraid of me, and even when they fall sick, they don't blame me. That's the secret of my success.

I don't want to harm anyone, but I am increasing year by year and humans are is responsible. If you desire to get rid of me, you must abandon all burning strategies and switch over to electrical alternatives. Will that be possible? Of course, if there is a will, there is a way. The dead leaves lying scattered in the fields are burnt to make ash which is an excellent fertilizer, but when these leaves decay and mix with the soil we get a better fertilizer.

Another question may crop up. How can we cook food without burning wood? That's where the relevance of smokeless oven comes in. A smokeless oven is made in such a way that they get only the necessary amount of oxygen to burn. It also saves fuel, and the Government is at present subsidizing the product. Can we do without motor vehicles? That will be difficult, but we can use a vehicle that does not emit much smoke. CNG vehicles emit less smoke. 4 stroke vehicles, diesel vehicles, two-stroke vehicles and vehicles which are not tuned will emit more smoke. Certain alternatives may be adopted to reduce pollution-prefer public transport, popularize electric vehicles, develop technical strategies to reduce and control pollution from factory chimneys. Increase of worldly comforts automatically increases the adverse impacts of it on ecology. Don't ignore me as just ordinary smoke because I'm dangerous and will appear before you as a silent killer. Prevention is better than cure, so if we are careful and take the necessary steps, we need not regret.

20

Red Alert

I am a newcomer to Kerala, and I was warmly welcomed by Estate owners. Some people use me to become rich, while others end their life because of me. I don't know whether I'm good or bad for society, but one thing, I'm certain is that I'm dangerous. I am of English origin, and I came into the market with the help of a multinational company. Many people have given me pet names like paraquet or gramasone. I destroy weeds as I am a powerful poison capable of drying up the weeds. Therefore, I am known as weed destroyer or pesticide. Generally, weeds are a big headache to the farmer because if weeds are not destroyed, farming will not be successful. It's difficult to get labourers to clear weeds owing to labour problems, so my arrival was an easy solution to this problem because I was able to do the work of twenty labourers in one day. I was widely used to destroy the weeds in the paddy fields and the rubber plantations in the estates. Farmers love me because weeds are removed at a low cost and without labour problems. In 1987, the company made a profit of 500 million dollars from me. Not only in England but in other countries too some factories manufacture me. Profit-making farmers are very fond of me and make use of my services. I had the opportunity to visit all the countries because I was popular throughout the world. Suddenly, I had a setback. In 1981, I was banned in Norway, in 1983 New Zealand and Sweden and in 1986 England. I would set it right. But in this context, you must be aware of the arguments against me by noted ecologists.

Once I enter the human body, there is no antidote. Those who want to commit suicide take me. According to statistics annually 1300 people in Japan and 1200 in Malaysia make use of me. When I'm sprayed, I enter the human body through the lungs and skin. I am known for causing bleeding when I enter through the nose. If I fall into the eye, it will lead to blindness those who continuously spray me will have a problem with the nails. In Columbia, supervisors entrust the labourers with the task of spraying me. When they come once a month to check the labourers, they can easily find out by observing the nails of the labourers who have done their duty. I also affect the functioning of the liver and kidneys.

Recently I was lavishly sprayed in the rubber estate with the result that ten cows of the labourers died and that's how reports about me came into the limelight. When I'm sprayed on the rubber plantations during the rainy season, I will mix with the rivers and water table and enter the human body. According to research reports, all chemicals cause cancer. But I act immediately, unlike the other chemicals that gradually cause cancer.

After hearing my story, you can decide. Isn't it better to avoid using me for making a profit and harming the earth? So, take courage to avoid using me, and that will be the best answer to my manufacturers.

21

This water will not quench your thirst

I am loved by all, the young and the old, the rich and the poor. I am present everywhere from the King's palace to the poor man's hut. My presence adds a royal touch to any function, and my existence is appreciated in star hotels as well as *paan* shops. I am very much in demand, especially during the summer. Do you know who I am. I'm cola. I belong to a big family. Coca-Cola, Pepsi cola, Fanta, sprite, thumps up etc. are some of my family members. Multinational companies make most of these. You may ask which is the best, but before I answer that I would like you to know the truth. First, you must understand the real intention of these multinational companies; their real intention is to make a profit and not to satisfy your thirst. When we drink one bottle, we will crave for the next. I have been put into the market with certain chemicals added to increase this craving. This is the truth and when people become aware of this truth, will the company be able to make a profit?

Our manufacturers are aware of human psychology, most people are deceived by TV advertisements. The company makes sure that I come in most of the advertisements. They sponsor popular games like cricket to popularize me. When I appear several times on TV those who sit in front of the TV for 10-12 hours watching their favourite stars and leaders drinking me, they too begin to crave for cola. In this way, my popularity increases day by day, and the company makes a huge profit.

Do you know what I contain? I contain phosphoric acid, or citric acid, caffeine, sugar, preservatives, colouring agents (chemicals) and a secret formula. To make me thick brominated vegetable oil is added. When the news spread that this would cause cancer, the company denied using this ingredient. I am an acidic drink. If you immerse a tooth in cola for a couple of hours, it will lose weight. It has been reported that those who drink cola regularly have worn out teeth. Cola also reduces the appetite and children who like cola tend to have very poor appetite. In cola there is no protein fat, vitamin or minerals; only food provides nutrition. The growth of children

will be affected if they don't take enough food. Sodium Benzoate used as a preservative in this is not good for people with heart problems. According to medical reports, caffeine creates many problems, and research studies prove that the colouring chemicals used in cola cause cancer. So now I'm sure you are quite aware of the dangers of consuming me regularly. Certain health workers have begun their propaganda against me, by popularizing drinks like tender coconut water, buttermilk etc. The public strongly influenced by ads will not believe anything against me. Whoever drinks me will thirst again and will fall ill. The moment this realization comes on people, I'll be out once and for all.

22

Tastemaker

I have no quality by myself. There's a general notion that when some people join a movement it flourishes whereas in the case of some people the movement is doomed. Likewise, I belong to the first category because when I mix with others, their qualities become better.

Lay people call me Ajinomoto, but science students call me monosodium glutamate or MSG. In the past older women with a passage of time became masters of tasty dishes. But today anyone can cook delicious meals with my help. When I'm added to any dish, I make it extremely tasty. Individual dishes like fried rice or noodles cannot be prepared without my help. All people like delicious food, which explains the great rush in hotels and bakeries. Wherever there is taste I'm there, I'm in high demand. But unfortunately, my selfless service is not acknowledged. Moreover, currently, I'm seen as a villain by some people.

Let me relate an incident that occurred in 1968, which will illustrate this. In America, a doctor named Robert began to experience numbness in his hands and legs. But specialists were unable to diagnose his disease. At the same time, another patient also happened to experience the same symptoms. Doctors began to study the history of both the patients, and they found out that both of them relished tasty food and used to take food from the Chinese restaurant. The doctors then extended their research to Chinese restaurants and found that they used Ajinomoto to augment the tastes of dishes. That's how I became the cause of Dr Robert's illness. The disease is known as Chinese Restaurant Syndrome (CRS).

Too much of anything is not good. I'm not very problematic if I'm used in small quantity. Water is good, but if you drink too much, you may die. Similarly, salt is good, but if you take forty spoons, death is sure. Anything that enters the body is not problematic up to a specific limit, but if it exceeds that it may prove

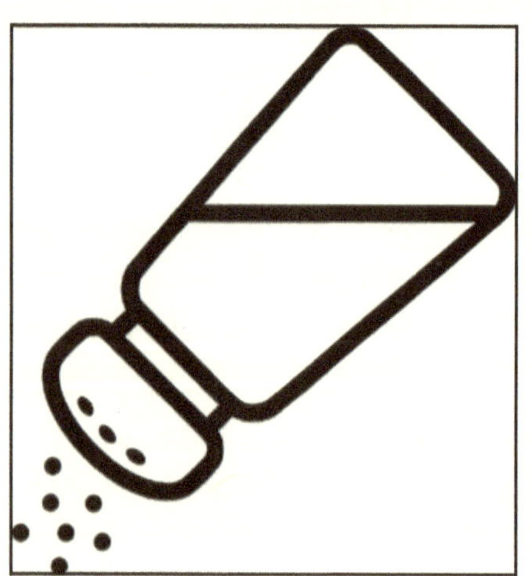

fatal. The scientific name for this level is known as the tolerance level, which will vary according to the individual's weight. Sometimes there may be instructions like, 'not for children below 12 years which means I will be harmful to children. Now there is a lot of propaganda against me. A group of scientist claim that I destroy the cells in the brain of children, and if this is ignored, it will lead to severe problems later in life. In countries like Malaysia and England foodstuffs in which

Ajinomoto is used, carry the warning 'not for children'. In 1971 an experiment was conducted in Japan. Food which contained 26% of Ajinomoto was given to children. The brain and nerves of the children were affected. In 1983 a research report from Japan stated that I was a cause for cancer.

Now I'm sure that you have understood how dangerous I'm. Those who give too much importance to tastes are likely to fall ill. So, isn't it better to eat natural products without chemicals and live a longer life? Prevention is better than cure.

23

Salt and Water

I am very often present in your body, though you are entirely unaware of it. I am **sodium nitrite.** As we share a common bacteria, people tend to mistake us. Though I look like common salt, my task is to act as a preservative, to prevent food from decaying. In the previous century, my services were explicitly used for the curing of meat, as I give out a pleasant smell and colour and softness as well and prevent decay. In the meat, there are deadly microbes called **Clostridium botulinum** and help to prevent these microbes from growing. My role in the flesh is significant. But some merchants misuse me. In Cold storages, where sales are low, they preserve meat with my help.

Recently there have been moves against me. According to a scientific study, sodium nitrate is dangerous for even a healthy person, because the veins dilate, BP drops, and oxidize the hemoglobin in the blood. When the power to carry oxygen is destroyed, it results in **Methemoglobinemia**. If it occurs in babies, there will be a colour change. This disease is known as a blue syndrome. Another finding is that when I'm used in non-vegetarian food, my character itself changes. I change into a chemical known as Nitrosoamine, which is cancer-causing. Vegetarians may tend to think that they are safe because I'm used only for meat. But that's a wrong notion because I'm present in fertilizers used for plants. After they absorb nitrogen, the remaining part will be washed into the wells and rivers and will enter the human body through the drinking water.

So, vegetarians cannot escape.

As the saying goes, the one who eats the salt will have to drink water and face the consequences. If I enter your body, you will

not only have to drink water but also become sick and take medicine. My advice is to avoid foods that use such chemicals.

Farmer's Friend

I am the earth's plower, but unfortunately, no one pays attention to me, and I feel hurt. It's quite natural that people who serve society wish to be recognized, but very often they are ignored.

You may wonder who I am, I'm an earthworm and in some people's view a despicable creature. But whether I'm condemned or ignored, my task is to serve you, while you sleep, my task is to make tunnels. I'm afraid of daylight, and as soon as day dawns, I hide in these tunnels. Moreover, some birds are fond of eating me, so hiding in these tunnels is mainly in self-defence. I make tunnels not just for the fun of it but for my livelihood. Just like farmers ploughing in the field, I plough with my body. Therefore, I'm known as nature's plower.

In the course of my ploughing, I also find my food, organisms, harmful bacteria, microbes etc. After digesting this, I excrete. I perform the function of the human intestine. That's why Aristotle the Greek Philosopher called the earthworm the earth's gut, I'm known as the farmer's friend because by making tunnels I'm doing the work of a plower. These tunnels provide air circulation, which is suitable for farming. Individual organisms in the soil cannot be directly absorbed by plants, I eat these organisms, digest and excrete it in a form that plants can easily absorb – elements such as nitrogen, phosphorus, potassium, calcium, magnesium. Destroying harmful microbes in the soil is itself a great thing.

Along with my excreta, I release a substance into the soil, which enables the earth to retain its nutrients. Now I'm sure you have understood my role in enriching the soil, and that's why I'm called the farmer's friend. I'm the yardstick to measure the richness of the earth. It's the presence of humic acid in my excreta that gives the vibrant dark colour to the soil, and this dark soil produces a good yield. But unfortunately, I'm not acknowledged by society for this good service.

Today farmers prefer chemicals and pesticides. When chemical farming is done continuously over a period, the saltiness and acidity of the soil will increase, I cannot survive in such conditions. If I'm put in saltwater, I will die within minutes. When chemical fertilizers are used, I will not be present, other microbes will disappear too. Consequently, the soil will become infertile and as a result when plants begin to wither, the farmers realized their mistake and reduced chemical fertilizers. Moreover, they began to popularize organic farming, and I was reinstated in a new form 'vermicompost'. Now farming using vermicompost has become very popular, and people who had hitherto considered me ugly and unclean began to acknowledge my valuable role in nature. It's not only me but all creatures in nature that have a distinctive role to play in maintaining the eco-balance. When this truth is ignored, it results in ecological catastrophes. It's for precisely this reason that serious efforts are being made all over the world to protect biodiversity. The need of the hour is to understand that every creature has an intensive purpose and a specific role to play in balancing this eco-system.

25

Let me alone

Everyone is fond of cashew nuts, and we are keen on its production because of its export value and the income it generates. In Kasargod district of Kerala, there are over three thousand hectares of cashew tree plantations. For a good yield, the cashew tree must overcome many threats. I am widely made use of to destroy the pests that decrease the yield and the owners of these plantations have acknowledged my skill and have been utilizing my services for the past two decades.

You may wonder who I am; I am none other than Endosulfan and I am an effective remedy, farmers sprayed me aerially, and now I'm spreading through the atmosphere. But of late, my future is in danger; I have now become controversial as several people from Kasargod have confronted me openly. Their accusations are based on specific health issues erupting in Kasargod district. There has been a steep rise in the cases of birth deformities, deformities due to poor nervous system functioning and skin problems. In most of the houses in Kasargod, there are many cases of adults and children being paralyzed. The consensus is that all these issues are the result of the abuse of Endosulfan and the amount of Endosulfan sprayed is very high.

Some argue that the culprit is not only Endosulfan. I am less poisonous when compared to my other family members, DDT, endrin, BHC etc. I have been banned in six countries, and  there is restricted use in 21 countries. According to certain reports, the impact of Endosulfan even for a short period on human beings is manifested by dizziness, vomiting, skin problems, migraine, anemia, breathing difficulty etc. As immunity will decrease with protein deficiency, the poor are more prone to this disease. Those who favour me argue that this is the only possibility and that there is no clear evidence that these diseases are the result of Endosulfan poisoning.

In the backdrop of this controversy, certain truths have come to the limelight, which everyone ought to know – every three years, the pesticides should be changed. In Kasargod, district Endosulfan was used continuously for more than two decades. People generally use pesticides without seriously reading the instructions and impacts given on the packets. Through organic farming and crop rotation, we can quickly reduce the use of chemicals. But unfortunately, no one takes this seriously.

Common sense tells us that it's not right to practice aerial spraying in thickly populated areas and where there are open wells. Do you think it is right to use me for twenty-two years at a stretch without reviewing? Am I responsible for using me without observing the rules? Moreover, will anyone in the world blindly trust someone or something for twenty-two years? Is it my fault? Obey laws and kindly let me alone.

26

My Story

The world moves because of me and no one can move from one place to another without me. It was with my advent that travel has become more comfortable and moreover. I'm proud that countries are bargaining for me. Can you guess who I am? I am called Diesel. Majority of vehicles prefer me, especially big vehicles. Motor manufacturers, as well as buyers/customers, prefer diesel vehicles because it's cheaper than petrol. It's a matter of pride for me that people depend on me. There is a saying that popularity breeds enemies. That's exactly what happened in my case. Many accusations have been levelled at me, some are true, but let us examine the allegations.

When there is fire, I cannot be seen, I'll change into hundreds of things you may be surprised to hear that almost four hundred and fifty chemicals have been found in the exhaust pipes of diesel vehicles, and many of them are cancer-causing. Some chemicals may cause respiratory disorders. The greatest impact will be on children, as they go to school in diesel vehicles. You might have observed that when the final school bell rings, the drivers will start the engines ready for departure and as the children board the bus, they will unknowingly inhale all the chemicals. The same thing happens in the bus stands, the whole area is polluted by the smoke that is emitted though these exhausted pipes. As children breathe fast, they inhale all these chemicals, and their lungs don't have the power to withstand the pollution. When many buses start their ignition together, the whole area becomes badly polluted. The drivers and the children are quite unaware of this pollution and its consequences. In some children, the impact of this will be seen only much later in life.

In motor vehicles, the danger will vary from vehicle to vehicle. The smoke from old diesel vehicles will contain a greater amount of chemicals. The chemicals that are emitted when the fuel burns are highly dangerous. Though I have an adverse impact,

for transportation purposes, I'm inevitable. If I'm abandoned on the grounds of pollutions, what will be the alternative?

We are in a dilemma because we have no other alternatives. So, our immediate task is to find out certain solutions, so the need of the hour is to conscientize people regarding certain things. Drivers and children should understand the hazardous effect of diesel smoke. Drivers should take care not to start the vehicles until they are ready to leave. Old vehicles should be abandoned. Sitting on the last seat should be avoided. Liquid Natural Gas (LNG) and Comprisal Natural Gas CNG) must be popularized. The Government must also be ready to support them. Children should not be allowed to stand close to the exhaust pipes.

Ecologists have an eye on the exhaust pipes of vehicles. Studies published by Yale University in February 2002 has adversely affected my future. They have reported that diesel smoke emissions can cause respiratory disorders in children. Do you think it's right to make me controversial? I was living peacefully under the earth, but you brought me out as a fuel. If you want my service, I must burn and when I burn, I emit smoke. You might have heard of people who create a problem when they set out to help others, my fate is just the same.

Appendix - 1

CSI & Eco-ministries

1. Since 1992

2. In the CSI Constitution → Mission of CSI Includes 'STEWARDSHIP OF CREATION'

3. Honored by United Nation's Development Programme & Alliance for Religions and Conservation

Awarded by Ban Ki Moon on November 3, 2009

CSI's Environment Programmes

1. Eco-Bible Study

2. World Environment Day

3. Ecological Sunday

4. Green Diocese, Parish, School Awards

5. Eco-Activists & Missionaries

6. Promoting Eco-friendly Constructions

7. Organizing Eco-Seminars, Conferences

8. Green Clergy & Teachers' Fellowships

9. Organic Farming

10. Responding to Govt. Policies related to Ecology

GREEN SCHOOL PROGRAMME

1. Resource Efficient Building

    a. Uses very little water
    b. Optimizes Energy Efficiency
    c. Minimizes Waste Generation
    d. Catches & Recycles Water
    e. Provides Healthier Space

2. Green School Programme is a Programme of **Centre for Environment Science.** CSI is PARTNERING.

3. They have a Curriculum (6 Subjects)

    a. Air
    b. Energy
    c. Food
    d. Land
    e. Water
    f. Waste
    g. Land

4. Methodology

    a. Each School will have one Coordinator and 6 Teachers to teach above 6 Syllabus

b. All have to complete the Course and upload reports on website before Oct. 30

c. Best School from all over India will be selected and awarded by Centre for Environment & Science

d. CSI Eco-Awards too will be decided based on the same norms.

5. GREEN SCHOOLS NETWORK all over India will be formed of which CSI School too will be part

BENEFITS

1. Focuses more on practice than theory

2. Monitoring is participatory & transparent

3. Helps Schools to record their available resources

4. Helps Schools to skillfully manage their resources

5. Equips resourceful teachers to foster environment literacy

6. Information after Audit can be shared

7. Students learn their usual subjects…with interest and ecological focus

SPIRITUAL COMMITMENT OF THE CHURCH

Appendix - 2

Books Published by CSI Synod Department of Ecological Concerns

1) **Reconciling with Nature (English, Telugu, Malayalam, Tamil, Kannada) 2002.** A Guide to a Green Church. Published by CSI SECC. Edited by Dr. Mathew Koshy Punnackad

2) **God is Green (2004) Ecological concerns and work of CSI Synod and Dioceses.** Published by CSI SECC. Edited by Dr. Mathew Koshy Punnackad

3) **Eco Vision and Mission (English and Tamil)2006.** A guide to Sunday School teachers, Contributors: Dr. Mathew Koshy Punnackad, Ms. Jessy Jeyakaran, Dr. Edwin Chandrasekharan, Published by CSI SECC

4) **A Christian Response to Ecological Crisis (2009)** Edited by Dr. Mathew Koshy Punnackad and Rt. Rev. Thomas Samuel Published jointly by CSI SECC and CSS

5)   **Green Gospel (2011)** Edited by Dr.Mathew Koshy Punnackad and Rt. Rev. Thomas Samuel, Published jointly by CSI SECC and CSS

6)   **Forest: Our Good Neighbour (2011)** A Worship Resource on 'Biodiversity', Published by CSI DEREC

7)   **Turn to God: Turn to Green (2012) A Worship Resource Book on 'Green Energy',** Published by CSI DEREC

8)   **Bread of Life: Bread for Life (2013) A Worship Resource Book on 'Food Justice',** Published by CSI DEREC

9)   **Word & World (2013) Bible Studies on Climate Justice** Published by CSI & BTESSC, Edited by Viji Varghese Eapen & Mohan Larbeer

10)   **Renewed Faith for a Redeemed Earth (2014) Eco-Theological Reflections,** Published by CSI, UTC & CSS, Edited by Viji Varghese Eapen & Allan Samuel Palanna

11)   **Green Church (2014)** Published by CSI SECC, Edited by Dr. Mathew Koshy Punnackad

12)   **Earth Bible Sermons 1 (2015) Ecological sermons** Published jointly by ISPCK and CSI, Edited by Dr. Mathew Koshy Punnackad

13)   **Earth Bible Sermons 2 (2015) Ecological sermons** Published jointly by ISPCK and CSI, Edited by Dr. Mathew Koshy Punnackad

14) **Earth Bible Sermons 3 (2016) Ecological sermons** Published jointly by ISPCK and CSI, Edited by Dr. Mathew Koshy Punnackad

15) **Green Parable (2016)** Edited by Dr. Mathew Koshy Punnackad

16) **Silent Rhythm. Eco tales for Children** (2017). Dr. Mathew Koshy Punnackad& Dr.Anne Susan Koshy Published jointly by ISPCK

17) **Silent Rhythm. Eco tales for Children(2019).** Dr. Mathew Koshy Punnackad & Dr.Anne Susan Koshy. Translated by Dr.Philip Robinson Published jointly by ISPCK and CSI

18) **Green Stories for Sunday School Children(2019).** Dr. Mathew Koshy Punnackad & Dr.Anne Susan Koshy. Published jointly by ISPCK and CSI

19) **Climate Emergency – Peoples Stories of Adaptation and Mitigation(2019).** Edited by Dr. Mathew Koshy Punnackad. Published jointly by CSI and ISPCK

20) **Sustainable living**. Edited by Dr. Mathew Koshy Punnackad. Published jointly by CSI and ISPCK

21) **Green Miracles** Edited by Dr. Mathew Koshy Punnackad. Published jointly by CSI and ISPCK.